W9-AAK-673

Stories
My
Grandfather
Should
Have
Told
Me

Stories
My
Grandfather
Should
Have
Told
Me

edited by Deborah Brodie
illustrated by Carmela Tal Baron

BONIM BOOKS
New York • London

Introductory matter © 1977 by Deborah Brodie
Illustrations © 1977 by Carmela Tal Baron

Library of Congress Cataloging in Publication Data
Main entry under title:

Stories my grandfather should have told me.

    CONTENTS: Glasgow, A. The pair of shoes.—Slobod-
kin, F. Names for sale.—Burstein, C. M. The wedding.
[etc.]
    1. Jews—Social life and customs—Juvenile fiction.
2. Short stories, Jewish. [1. Jewish way of life—
Fiction. 2. Short stories, Jewish] I. Brodie,
Deborah.
PZ5.S8843   [Fic]   76-48149
ISBN 0-88482-752-6

BONIM BOOKS
a division of Hebrew Publishing Company
80 Fifth Avenue
New York, N.Y. 10011

PRINTED IN THE UNITED STATES OF AMERICA

Acknowledgements

The publisher gratefully acknowledges permission to reprint the following copyrighted materials: "The Pair of Shoes" by Aline Glasgow, abridged from *The Pair of Shoes*, text copyright © 1971 by Aline Glasgow, reprinted by permission of the Dial Press; "Names for Sale" by Florence Slobodkin, from *Sarah Somebody*, copyright © 1969 by Florence and Louis Slobodkin, reprinted by permission of Vanguard Press, Inc.; "The Wedding" by Chaya M. Burstein, adapted from *Rifka Bangs the Teakettle*, copyright © 1970 by Chaya M. Burstein, reprinted by permission of Harcourt Brace Jovanovich, Inc.; "A Hebrew Village" by Devorah Omer, from *Rebirth*, copyright © 1972 by the Jewish Publication Society of America, reprinted by permission of the publisher; "The Little Heroes of Kfar Tabor," translated by Azriel Eisenberg and Leah Ain Globe, from *Sabra Children*, Jonathan David Publishers, copyright © 1970 by Azriel Eisenberg and Leah Ain Globe, reprinted by permission of the authors; "Waiting for Mama" by Marietta Moskin, from *Waiting for Mama*, copyright © 1975 by Marietta Moskin, reprinted by permission of Coward, McCann and Geoghegan, Inc.; "Ben Goes Into Business" by Marilyn Hirsh, adapted from *Ben Goes Into Business*, copyright © 1973 by Marilyn Hirsh, reprinted by permission of Holiday House, Inc.; "P'Idyon Ha-Ben" by Sydney Taylor, from *All-of-a-Kind Family Uptown*, copyright © 1958 by Sydney Taylor, reprinted by permission of Follett Publishing Company; "The House in the Tree" by Molly Cone, adapted from *The House in the Tree*, copyright © 1968 by Molly Cone, reprinted by permission of Thomas Y. Crowell Company, Inc.; "Miriam Lives in a Kibbutz" by Cordelia Edwardson, adapted from *Miriam Lives in a Kibbutz*, Lothrop, Lee and Shepard Company Publishers, copyright © 1969 by Anna Riwkin-Brick, reprinted by permission of William Morrow and Company, Inc.

"No, No, Not Haman," copyright © 1977 by Lilly S. Routtenberg, and "The Sticky Surprise," copyright © 1977 by David A. Adler, were written especially for *Stories My Grandfather Should Have Told Me*.

For my teacher, Rabbi Gershon Hadas,
as I promised.

D. B.

Contents

IN AMERICA, THE GOLDEN LAND

IN THE STATE OF ISRAEL

IN AMERICA TODAY

Foreword

The twelve stories in this collection explore the variety and richness of twentieth-century Jewish life—from the European *shtetl* to a contemporary American setting. In every story, children are active participants.

Making friends, building a tree house, acting in a play, sewing, baking, dancing, studying—these children emerge as exciting and resourceful individuals. With imagination and energy, they confront both the crises and the high points of everyday life.

When the young reader identifies with an appealing character or a compelling incident, he or she will discover the quality of Jewish life as seen through the eyes of other children. This is an educationally sound and extremely pleasant way to absorb Jewish values and concepts.

All of the selections in *Stories My Grandfather Should Have Told Me* have been tested for readability and appeal to young readers. These well-loved stories always evoke a response—sometimes a chuckle, sometimes a tear or nod of understanding.

How does it feel to have an about-to-be-married brother? To be the son of a famous father? What is it like to be the youngest child in a family, or the oldest? The reader responds, yes, that *is* the way I would feel.

The Jewish child who has attended a traditional Bar Mitzvah celebration, wedding, Purim festivity, or Passover Seder will recognize elements of personal experience. For other children, these stories can be an introduction to a body of knowledge and culture with universal elements which they can appreciate.

One of the advantages of an anthology is the freedom it affords young readers to pick and choose stories at random. Thus the needs and interests of more than one child in a family or class can be provided for in a book of selected stories. All of the stories lend themselves to the shared pleasure of reading aloud.

Once, when my daughter finished reading a particularly enjoyable book, she exclaimed, "Why aren't there more books like this one?" Indeed there are. For two years, I sifted through library collections on a "treasure hunt" for outstanding stories of Jewish life. The delightful illustrations by Carmela Tal Baron add a visual dimension to the vitality of the stories.

It was a joy to prepare this book for young readers. I hope they will let me know which stories were their favorites.

D. B.
New York City
Iyar, 5736
May, 1976

In a Little Jewish Town

The Pair of Shoes
by Aline Glasgow

This poor family in a little town in Poland had only a few treasured possessions: a set of holy books, a copper tea urn, a cow. In this family, there were two parents, two brothers, a sister—and only one pair of shoes.

How could Jacob celebrate his Bar Mitzvah without his own shoes to wear? What happened to make the sad and bitter father open his heart?

Once long ago, in a small house in the town of Gebernye in the country of Poland, there lived a mother, a father, three children, four chickens and a cow. But in this house there was only one pair of shoes.

Sara Rebecca, the mother, was thin, with worried eyes and yellow hair drawn into a knot. She did her work silently, moving through the house like a shadow. Sara Rebecca did not wear the pair of shoes. When she went to market, and even when she went to synagogue on Saturday, she wore only her pair of worn *pontussel.*

3

The father, Avrum, was a sickly man. His face was long and bony, and his black beard came down to his second shirt button. It was hard for the children to tell when their father was smiling at them, for his beard covered most of his mouth. So they looked not at his mouth, but at his eyes, and usually the eyes of Avrum were half-closed in prayer. Since Avrum could not walk, he had no need of the pair of shoes. He wore only slippers upon his crippled feet.

The house was separated into two rooms by a wide, heavy curtain. Both rooms were kept very clean, for the daughter, Dubbie, helped the mother. She swept, she scrubbed, she washed the dishes, and she made the beds. Each morning, too, it was her special task to polish the mother's one remaining treasure, the copper samovar, until it shone like a single candle in the poor bare home. Because she was the youngest, Dubbie had not yet used the pair of shoes. She went upon the hard-packed dirt floor in her bare feet.

Each morning, the younger brother, Noah, fed the four chickens with the few crumbs left from the table. He scooped up the warm, dusty eggs from the small coop beneath the great stove. He helped the mother in her vegetable garden. And he took care of Olga, his beloved cow. For his work Noah did not need the pair of shoes. But more and more, as he grew older, he needed them when he went to the rabbi for his studies.

It was the eldest, Jacob, who wore the pair of

shoes most of the time. He was almost thirteen, and he wore the pair of shoes when he went to the rabbi, when he went to the synagogue, and when he went into town to work at whatever odd jobs he could find.

When the shoes were new, they had been quite elegant, with eight shiny pearl buttons and a gray fur lining. They had belonged to Avrum, and he had worn them with pride. But that was long ago, before the accident had crippled him.

Today, years later, the family no longer spoke of the accident that had taken from them a father young and strong and had left to them a father crippled, brooding, and helpless. Only Avrum himself, once in a long while, would look at his wife and daughter and his two sons, piercing them with his heavy thoughtful eyes and saying, "The ways of the Lord are inscrutable. The accident which I thought would ruin my life has given to me my greatest joy. It took from me the use of my legs, but it gave me my holy books."

And to the children it bequeathed his pair of shoes. They were old shoes now, high and black and covered with deep creases of age, but they were warm shoes, and when Jacob polished them and shined the pearl buttons, it seemed to the three children that they were the handsomest shoes in all the world.

One night as Jacob sat lovingly rubbing the pair of shoes with his cloth, his father looked up from his books. For a moment his prayers ceased.

Through veiled eyes he stared at his elder son. Then, softly he asked, "Why is it, my son, that you rub the shoes so hard and so long?"

The boy looked away. In a hoarse voice he muttered, "Because a man is not a man unless he walks in shoes!"

The father's pale fingers plucked delicately at the fringes of his long tallis. "This is your belief?" he asked slowly.

Almost defiantly the boy replied, "This is my belief."

The father did not answer. In a moment the sound of his prayers hovered again above the small room like a circle of endless song. Bending his head, Jacob returned to his pair of shoes.

Later that night, while the children slept, the mother carefully poured tea for the father from her gleaming samovar. "Avrum," she sighed, "on the third Sabbath we will celebrate Jacob's Bar Mitzvah. What are we to do? The boy must have the pair of shoes for his own! It cannot be put off any longer!"

The room was very still now. Outside, the wind had begun to moan across the brown countryside.

"It can wait," said the father.

"Until when? Until when can it wait?"

"Until he has truly become a man," he replied, and for a moment he smiled with his brooding eyes.

On the very next morning the little sister came

to the mother. "There are only four candles for the Friday night holy service," said Dubbie. Sara Rebecca looked up from the stove. "Ai," she sighed, "it will be a good warm loaf of bread! And you shall have a piece as soon as you return from the town. See!" she cried, digging into the pocket of her apron. "See how lucky you are! I have found a kopeck for the candle! Now wrap your feet, for it's cold out!"

Dubbie looked at her mother. "No, Mama," she said, shaking her head back and forth. "I don't want to wrap my feet. Today I want to wear the pair of shoes!"

"The pair of shoes!" whispered the mother.

Dubbie looked down at her bare feet. "I am nine years old," she replied quietly. "I am too old to go into town without shoes any longer."

The mother did not answer. Instead she turned to Jacob.

"Jacob," she whispered, glancing anxiously toward the father, who sat, as always, bent over his holy book, "perhaps this morning you will not go to the town? Try instead to find work in one of the orchards."

"Why?" asked the boy.

"Because," replied the mother, "this morning your little sister needs the pair of shoes."

The older boy glared at his mother. "Why does she need them? She is too small to wear shoes yet. Besides, she is a girl."

The father lifted his eyes slowly from his

Talmud. He stared at his son. Then he returned to his prayers.

Jacob stood up. He took the shoes from the wooden box in which he kept them, and he handed them to his mother. Without another word, he climbed up onto the great stove and buried his head in his hands.

Sara Rebecca looked down at the pair of shoes. "Such small feet, *bebele,* and such big shoes!" Swiftly she began to stuff rags into the wide toes.

Holding her breath, Dubbie slipped her feet into the pair of shoes. The mother laced the strings tightly around the eight pearl buttons.

The little girl stood up. Her eyes shone as she exclaimed, "Mama! See how beautiful they look!"

"Shh," whispered Sara Rebecca, glancing again toward the table. "Come outside."

With a smile Dubbie waved to her mother and started down the dusty road, disappearing clumsily around the bend. For a long while, the mother stood by the door, staring after her. Suddenly a loud voice coming from the house made her start. She turned and walked inside.

Jacob stood facing his father, his cheeks pale with anger.

"But I *will* have those shoes for my own!" he cried. "I am no longer a child. The second Sabbath after this one coming will be the day of my Bar Mitzvah. Soon I will be apprenticed and then it is I who will bring bread into this house."

The father said never a word, only buried

himself more deeply in his Bible and his Talmud and his other holy books.

The mother rushed at her son. "Ai!" she cried. "Beg your father for his forgiveness!"

The boy turned away. "I will not beg my father," he muttered, and he left the room.

Later in the day, Sara Rebecca called her family to the afternoon meal of hot red borscht, cooked from the beets of her small garden, and potatoes, also from her garden.

"Ai," she sighed, as she sat down at the silent table. "Dubbie should have been home long ago."

When the meal was over, Noah's friend, Semyon, arrived. The younger boy turned to his mother. "How can I go to the rabbi for my lesson?" he asked. "Dubbie is not yet home with the pair of shoes."

Jacob stood up from the table, his eyes fixed upon the dirt floor. "I will look for her up the road," he said. Without waiting for an answer, he ran out of the house.

It was only a short while after, as the mother was clearing away the dishes and pouring the boiling tea for the father, that Jacob returned, with Dubbie in his arms.

"See, Mama," cried the little girl, her words tumbling between laughter and tears. "I didn't drop the candle! But isn't it silly? I twisted my ankle!" She continued quickly in a high, thin voice, "It was a stone in the road that made me fall, Mama . . . not the shoes."

All through that troubled night the mother and

father sat by the little girl. They spoke to her
soothingly. They held her close. The father
prayed. But in the morning she was no better. The
ankle was swollen and red.

"Ai, Mama!" cried the feverish girl. "How my
foot aches!"

The mother stood up. She turned to her eldest
son. "You must fetch the doctor from town," she
said.

Jacob, who was almost a grown man, asked
quickly, "With what will we pay the doctor?"

And Noah, who was still a boy, said slowly,
"We could sell Olga, the cow."

The mother shook her head. "No," she said,
"we will not sell Olga. How can we sell a dear
friend? We will sell the samovar."

Everyone grew quiet. Even Dubbie stopped
her ceaseless turning to stare at the mother as she
carefully lifted the shining samovar from its place
of honor in the center of the table. "For a long time
Semyon's mother has admired my samovar," she
said. "I know she will buy it. Take it to her, Jacob,
and then go to Dr. Raikov in Gebernye."

Jacob put on the pair of shoes and took the
samovar from his mother. In a moment he was
gone.

All during that long morning, while the
mother tended to her work, the father did not stir
from his daughter's bedside. The gaunt, silent man
sat bent over the little girl, softly stroking her moist
hair.

"I will read you a story from the Bible," he said hesitantly once in a low voice.

"No," whispered the child. "I am too tired. . . . "

She tossed, fell into a short sleep, then started up, crying and mumbling strange mixed words.

Once, toward the end of the morning, she sat up suddenly and smiled at Noah. "I would like to see Olga," she cried. "I love Olga. I love her milk." Then she fell back upon her pillow into a feverish sleep.

"Go," said the mother to Noah, "go and bring Olga from the shed."

And so later, when Jacob arrived in the doctor's droshky, he led the doctor into a small dark room in which a little girl lay on an old wooden bed, surrounded by a mother, a father, a brother, and a cow.

The doctor bent over his patient, pressing the hot swollen ankle with his firm hands. "The ankle is fractured," he said at last. "It will have to be set immediately or the leg will not grow right."

With skilled hands he set to work. The mother and Noah cried when they heard the little girl's screams, but the father and Jacob, though red-eyed, remained silent. Even Olga grew restless, as if she, too, understood.

After a long while the doctor spoke. "She will sleep now," he said. "I have given her something to make her rest." He stood up.

Sara Rebecca rose heavily. "Thank you, doctor," she said. "Please, before you leave, a cup

of hot tea. . ." Remembering suddenly that her
samovar was gone, the mother turned toward the
table. Then, in the next instant, when she saw the
beautiful copper samovar once more in its place of
honor, her sobs filled the room.

The doctor turned toward the father. Pale and
drawn, Avrum looked away. In a strained voice he
said, "Thank you, Doctor, for our daughter." Then
he looked at Jacob.

Quickly the boy drew two paper rubles from
his pocket and handed them to the doctor.

"Thank you," said the doctor. "There, there,
Mother, don't cry. In a month's time your little girl
will be running about the yard again. You will see!"
In a moment he was gone and the only sound that
could be heard in the small room was that of
Dubbie's slow, even breathing.

Filled with a great weariness, Sara Rebecca
asked in a hollow voice, "Where did you get the
money, Jacob? If you did not sell the samovar,
where did you get the rubles?"

Strangely, unexpectedly, the father's voice
rang in the silent room. "Look at the boy's feet,
Sara!"

The mother turned to look. Before her, upon
the hard-packed dirt floor stood her son, tall,
defiant, and barefoot. Wrenched by an unbear-
able pain, she whispered, "The pair of shoes. . . ."

"I sold them, Mama!" Jacob exclaimed. He
wheeled toward Noah, his eyes pleading.

For a moment Noah stared at his older

brother, horrified. Then solemnly he nodded.

"But," cried the mother hoarsely, "you were told to sell the samovar!"

Jacob stared down at the floor. "I decided to sell the pair of shoes instead."

His heavy-lidded gaze measuring Jacob, the father asked, "How then, my son, will you walk to your Bar Mitzvah on the third Sabbath?"

After a pause the boy replied, "I will walk in my bare feet."

"But, can a man walk without shoes and still be a man?" asked the father softly.

The boy looked down, "A man can walk without shoes and still be a man," he said.

The father spoke not another word, but turned once more to his books. Jacob sat down next to his sleeping sister. Noah led Olga into the shed. And Sara Rebecca, her eyes swollen, busied herself with the evening meal.

It was after the dishes had been cleared away and the mother was pouring the hot tea from the shining samovar that the father laughed. Dubbie, sitting up in bed now, her fever broken, looked at him in wonder. Never before had she heard her father laugh in this way.

Avrum turned to his elder son. "I have made a decision, Jacob," he said. From the pile of books that was always at his side he selected three, beautifully bound in gold.

"Tomorrow morning," he said, "you will go into Gebernye to the store of the moneylender, and you will sell these three books. Noah will go with you. From there you will go to the cobbler. You will tell him to make one pair of shoes for yourself and one for your brother. The money from the third book will be used to buy our Dubbie a pair of shoes—the kind that is meant for a girl to wear—when she is better."

Not even a sigh could be heard in the room.

Jacob watched intently as a hen strutted across the floor. Noah sat unmoving. Dubbie began to cry. And the mother stared at her husband as at a stranger, someone she must learn again to know and to understand.

Avrum, whose eyes had not left Jacob in all this time, smiled. "And on the Sabbath," he said firmly, "on the third Sabbath, my son, when you walk to your Bar Mitzvah, you will walk in your own pair of shoes."

Choosing each word with great care, Avrum turned to the mother. "The night before last, Sara, while the children slept, you asked me when Jacob would have his own pair of shoes." The mother lowered her eyes. The father continued, "It is said in the Talmud that there is a time for each boy to become a man. Now is the time for Jacob. Now he will have his own pair of shoes!"

"But how can you sell your holy books?" whispered the mother.

The father paused. "I learned something today," he said haltingly, "something I will never forget." He stopped, stretched his arms toward his family. Then, looking into each beloved face, he said, "And I did not learn it from my holy books. I learned it from my wife, my sons, and from my little daughter!"

Suddenly Jacob spoke. "I learned something, too," he said, a smile lighting his face. "And do you know . . . I learned it from an old, old pair of shoes!"

Names For Sale
by Florence Slobodkin

*Do you remember when you first learned to
read? Did you feel proud when you wrote your
own name for the first time?*

*Sarah felt like a real somebody. In the one-
room school in a little Polish town, her skill in
writing helped her show kindness to a poor class-
mate.*

The months went by and the weather grew
cool. The children now wore sweaters or jackets in
class. Miss Chesnov wore a navy blue suit that
came directly from Warsaw, Deborah said.

Then suddenly winter came. The wind howled
and the frost nipped Sarah's fingers. Miss Chesnov
lit a fire in the stove in the middle of the room.

She put in bits of wood and bricks of dried
turf. The fire burned slowly but gave off a pleasant
warmth. After a while the children sitting close to
the fire would feel too warm and take off their
sweaters, while those at the outer edge of the circle

17

got less of the fire's warmth and still felt the chill in the air.

One very cold day the fire did not burn well. Miss Chesnov went to call her father.

Mr. Chesnov looked at the fire and said, "There is nothing wrong. You are not using enough turf. More turf will make a bigger blaze and the room will be warm."

Then he turned to the children.

"Tell your parents that during the winter you must bring two kopecks every Monday. That will pay for the turf we must buy to keep you warm. Now, don't forget. I will be at the door on Monday morning to collect the two kopecks."

Another two kopecks a week!

"That makes eight more kopecks a month," groaned Mama. "Well, we will manage."

Sarah sighed with relief. How she would have hated to meet Mr. Chesnov at the door on Monday and have to say, "I do not have the two kopecks for the turf."

But there was one child who had to do just that.

Luba was a stout, sad-faced girl. On Monday Luba was stopped at the door.

"Where are your two kopecks?" asked Mr. Chesnov.

Luba did not answer.

"You do not have the money?" asked Mr. Chesnov.

"No," whispered Luba.

"When will you bring it?"

"I don't know."

Mr. Chesnov pulled at his beard thoughtfully.

"Well," he said, "you have paid four gulden, so you may come in. But you have not paid for the warmth in this room. Where do you sit?"

Luba pointed to the bench in front of Sarah.

"That is a warm bench," said Mr. Chesnov. "That is for a child who pays for the turf. Here is where you will sit now."

Mr. Chesnov pulled a chair to the outskirts of the room, as far as possible from the stove.

"Sit here," he said.

Fortunately, it was early in the morning. None of the other children except Sarah had arrived. Sarah was too embarrassed for Luba to look at her, and later, all through the lessons, she thought of Luba sitting far from the stove.

Every morning at ten o'clock Miss Chesnov went to the back room for a glass of tea while the children stayed in the classroom. That was their recess.

One day Naomi brought a notebook to Sarah.

"Will you write my name in my brand new book?" she asked. "Your handwriting is so beautiful . . . even Miss Chesnov says so."

"Of course," said Sarah, and wrote "Naomi" in her cousin's book.

"Now write my name," said Deborah, holding out her book.

Sarah started to say, "Of course," when she

noticed that Luba had left her seat in the far corner
of the room and was warming herself at the fire. As
soon as Miss Chesnov returned she would go quickly back to her place in the cold.

"Will you write my name, Sarah?" asked
Deborah again.

Deborah was the daughter of the only rich
man in the village.

"She can bring two kopecks every week without any trouble, while poor Luba . . ." thought
Sarah.

Suddenly she had an idea.

"Deborah," she said, "I will write your name
very carefully and very beautifully . . . if you will
pay me a kopeck."

Deborah laughed. "One kopeck! Well, that's a
bargain. Write my name and here is a kopeck
waiting for you."

She took the coin out of her apron pocket and
showed it.

Sarah began to write. Since she was to be paid
for it, she wrote especially carefully. Deborah was
pleased and paid the kopeck.

"I have a kopeck. Write my name," said Judith.

"Write mine, too," said Leah, and then Esther.

By the time Miss Chesnov came back, Sarah
had earned four kopecks!

"What are you going to do with all that money?" whispered Naomi.

Sarah put the four kopecks into her little bag
and pinned it inside her apron pocket, and just
smiled.

When school was over that day Sarah whispered to Luba, "Here are four kopecks. Tomorrow give two of them to Mr. Chesnov and keep the other two for next week."

"They're yours. I don't want them," protested Luba.

But Sarah pressed the coins into her hand.

"Maybe I'll earn some more the same way," she said. "Take them."

Luba shivered a little and took the money.

For the next two weeks she sat near the fire. And although there were weeks after that when Luba could not pay the two kopecks (because Sarah had not been asked to write anyone's name), there were many weeks when Sarah was able to give Luba the money to pay for a seat near the fire.

The Wedding
by Chaya M. Burstein

Rifka will miss her older brother Velvl when he gets married and moves to another town. Will she like his bride, Fraydeh? Rifka is all set to be angry with her.

This story takes place in Russia over seventy years ago. Many of the same customs are still observed at Jewish weddings today: fasting before the ceremony, a wedding canopy, reading of the marriage contract, dancing, singing—and of course, tears of joy.

The aching, itching guests climbed down from the wagon, to be greeted by little round Reb Sender, Velvl's father-in-law, and by other relatives, with a flurry of, "Welcome, come in . . . rest and wash up from your long journey . . . have some breakfast."

"Where did Velvl go?" Rifka asked Elli.

He shrugged. "Don't worry. He'll be back in time to get married. I'm hungry! When do we eat?"

The next few hours were spent in washing up,

combing and braiding hair, dressing in wedding
finery, eating and drinking.

"Rifkalleh." Mama called her over. "Make sure
that the children behave at the table."

"But where is Velvl, Mama?"

"We won't see him again until the wedding
ceremony. He is reading in the holy books now,
and he'll be fasting all day long. Fraydeh will be
fasting all day, too."

"Why should they be hungry when they're
supposed to be happy?" Rifka was puzzled.

"They're supposed to be thinking about their
new responsibilities to each other and to God.
Fasting always helps people to think more seri-
ously."

"Not me!" Elli butted in. "It just makes me
think of my stomach."

Rifka and Raizelleh, as the two oldest girls at
the children's end of the table, became the police-
men.

"Elli, stop grabbing the jelly."

"Don't wipe the butter on your dress, Tova."

"Zev and Elli—stop tickling each other!"

"Berelleh, you'll choke if you eat three rolls at
once!"

Suddenly, Rifka saw Elli disappearing under
the table. She grabbed his ankle and dragged him
out.

"If you do that once more," she whispered
fiercely, "I'm going to tell Reb Mendl about the
time you untied his shoelaces!"

Elli turned white and then red and then sat meekly down on the bench, not stirring until it was time to go to the wedding hall.

As the entire company walked down the smoothly paved main street of Belta, music floated out of the wedding hall ahead and tickled their feet. Raizelleh and Rifka danced as they walked, and Zev and Elli began to gallop and whinny.

"Behave yourselves!" Mama ordered again.

They opened the door and were greeted by a blast of music that made their ears tingle.

"Welcome to the bridegroom's family and guests," the people in the hall called out, and they were surrounded and greeted by silkily rustling ladies and dignified black-suited men and giggling children.

A great chandelier blazed in the center of the hall, shining down on the crowding guests. The little band of musicians struck up a lively polka. Violins squeaked, the bass fiddler sawed back and forth energetically, and the clarinet gaily led the melody. Elli and Zev began to jump again.

Rifka had eyes only for the raised platform at the far end of the room. There, sitting on a high-backed red velvet chair, was a slender girl, dressed all in white. In the middle of the music, noise, and bustle of happy people, only the bride looked quiet and thoughtful. Rifka felt a rush of sympathy for Fraydeh, even though she had been ready to hate her.

As the adult guests were introduced, Rifka

waited and watched the young bride. She was as
pale as Velvl had been on the morning he was
called to read the Bible in the synagogue. Her large
dark eyes glowed below her black, braided hair.

"Rifkalleh," she said, smiling past the grownups and reaching out her hand. "Velvl has told me
so much about you. I'm so glad that now you will
be my sister, too."

Rifka stood silent, tongue-tied by shyness.
Raizelleh pushed her forward, and she stumbled
up to Fraydeh's chair.

"I never had a sister," she mumbled, her eyes
downcast.

"Neither did I," Fraydeh answered, "just two
brothers. And I always wanted a sister."

She leaned over quickly and kissed Rifka.

The rest of the afternoon passed in a rosy glow
of happiness for Rifka. The band played with
gusto. She polkaed with Raizelleh and pranced
about with Elli and swung Berelleh into the air
while he screamed with delight. Her pink dress
and Raizelleh's blue dress flared out as they spun
breathlessly.

"Like two beautiful flowers." Mama sighed
and blew her nose.

Fraydeh's words, "I always wanted a sister,"
went singing through Rifka's mind as she danced.
She stole glances at Velvl's sweet-faced bride whenever she could. How could she ever have been
angry at Fraydeh?

Gradually, the dance music slowed down. Only

the violins carried a slow, thoughtful melody. The guests stepped back, murmuring, "It's time for the veiling ceremony."

Mama, Fraydeh's mother, Aunt Miriam, and the other women of the family placed themselves in two lines beside Fraydeh's chair. All eyes turned to the door. Velvl entered the room, splendid in his new black suit and his squeaky shoes. Papa and Fraydeh's father, who carried a white lace veil, were beside him.

They walked slowly between the two lines of women, up to Fraydeh's chair. Then Velvl placed the veil over Fraydeh's glossy hair and covered her face.

Suddenly, the music burst out loudly. The women joined hands to dance in a circle around Fraydeh's chair. Rifka and Raizelleh ran up to join the circle and discovered that tears were running down Mama's and Fraydeh's mother's face as they stamped and hopped around the bride.

Twirling his sticks, the drummer stood up and set a marching rhythm—bam, bam, bam—which made his plump cheeks and his black beard quiver. The women stopped dancing and wiped their streaming faces.

All the men gathered in a large group around Velvl. The band of musicians lifted their instruments and, playing a lively march, followed the drummer down the center of the hall and out the door. The bridegroom and all the other men and boys marched happily after the music makers.

"Where are we going?" asked Rifka.

"Now we go to the wedding canopy," Mama answered, dabbing her eyes again. "May I live to walk beside you to the wedding canopy also, my child."

The women clustered around the white-veiled bride and followed the men out of the hall and down the twilit street to the synagogue.

Townspeople leaned out of their windows, waving and admiring the bride and groom. Rifka and Raizelleh marched proudly to the music, pulling Berelleh between them.

In the synagogue courtyard, Uncle Ephraim and Velvl's best friend Mottel—his face wistful—stood waiting with two other men. Each held a pole that supported one corner of the canopy, a square of satin fabric.

Aunt Miriam sighed. "Ah, the bridal canopy."

"Why is there a bridal canopy?" Rifka asked.

"This is a roof of cloth, which is a symbol of the home that Velvl and Fraydeh will build together," Aunt Miriam explained. "Now hush, the ceremony is beginning," and she began to sob noisily into her handkerchief.

Velvl and Fraydeh stood side by side under their make-believe roof, and the guests gathered around them. Rifka saw Fraydeh's dark eyes shining through the white lace as the erect, white-bearded rabbi read the wedding contract.

All was quiet except for the voice of the rabbi and the weeping of some of the guests. When the

reading was finally done, Velvl and Fraydeh, in
soft voices, agreed to the terms of the contract.
Then the cantor sang a blessing over the wine, and
Velvl lifted his bride's veil. They each took a sip of
wine from the cup that the rabbi held.

The cup was thrown to the ground, and the
tinkling sound it made as it smashed also broke the
quiet, solemn mood. Everybody exploded into
backslapping and embraces.

Mama hugged Fraydeh. Fraydeh's mother
smothered Rifka with a great wet kiss, Papa embraced Velvl, who embraced Reb Sender. When
Elli rushed up to pull at his big brother's jacket,
Velvl forgot his new husbandly dignity and
snatched Elli up and swung him into the air.

"Congratulations! A long life to you both!"
everybody called out, laughing and crying at the
same time.

Rifka squeezed in between the ladies and
kissed Fraydeh joyfully; then she skipped back to
her friend.

"Raizelleh," she exclaimed, "now *I* have a
sister, too."

Raizelleh grinned down at Tova, who stood
timidly close beside her. "That's not all good,
Rifka."

Suddenly, the clarinet and the violins, the
drum, and the bass fiddle set up a rollicking dance
tune. Reb Sender shouted to be heard above the
uproar of voices and instruments.

"Honored guests," he called, "now it's time to

celebrate. The bride and groom will lead us back
to the wedding hall for a wedding feast. Let's eat
and drink and dance in honor of the marriage of
Reb Mosheh's Velvl to my daughter, Fraydeh.
May they have a long and happy life together!"

"Amen," the guests responded heartily.

In the Land of Israel

A Hebrew Village
by Devorah Omer

*For centuries, Hebrew was the language of
prayers and holy books. While the settlers in Pal-
estine worked to make the barren land bloom,
Eliezer Ben-Yehudah struggled to make Hebrew
the modern, living language of the country. He
created new words and, in 1910, began to publish
several volumes of a dictionary. He dreamed of
making Hebrew the official language of the Jewish
state that would someday be established.*

*Ben-Zion admired his father, Eliezer Ben-Ye-
hudah. It wasn't easy for Ben-Zion to be the son of
an outspoken and determined man, but he did
enjoy hearing his "abba" praised by the Hebrew-
speaking people of a village they visited. He also
had fun on an odd train ride interrupted by angry
Arab horsemen.*

Ben-Zion sat in front, next to the driver, with a
whip in his hand, thrilled at being able to point out
the way. This was the third time he was leaving
Jerusalem by carriage.

33

After many hours of plodding along in the sands of the lowlands, Eliezer suddenly called out, "Look over there. A red roof. That must be the synagogue of Rishon-le-Zion. We are almost there."

When they reached the village, his wife, Chemdah, was filled with surprise. This was not the village she had visualized. She saw white, blue, and pink houses—like flowers planted in rows in a garden. The dry, sandy scenery had changed as if by magic, and everything here was fresh and green. Vines and trees grew in abundance.

"This is the Hebrew village!" Eliezer announced formally. "This is our soil. The desert has become a place of habitation!"

"Where are these people going, Abba?" asked Ben-Zion, pointing at the men who were walking in one direction with parcels in their hands.

"They are going to the public bath, to get washed and ready for the Sabbath. It will soon be Sabbath, my son. Well, we've arrived. Here is David's house, where we are going to spend the Sabbath."

They passed a group of children who were playing with a ball. Ben-Zion stopped to watch them for a moment.

"Abba!" he called out, when he caught up with his father. "They are playing in Hebrew! I heard them call out to one another—'Let me have it!' 'Catch!' 'It's your turn now!' " Ben-Zion's face shone as if he had discovered a big treasure.

"Yes, my son," replied his father. "Here, in Rishon-le-Zion, a generation of Hebrew-speaking

children is being raised. One day all the children
and adults in this country will speak only Hebrew.
In Rishon, they are taking the first steps on this
long and difficult journey."

Friday evening was spent with the family of
David, the village teacher. After supper the house
was filled with guests. They all wanted to meet
Ben-Yehudah, about whom they had heard so
much. To Eliezer's delight, everybody spoke only
Hebrew.

In the beginning Ben-Zion listened to the talk
about the village of Haderah and its terrible fate—
how all its inhabitants had died of malaria and
nobody was left there at all—and how the place
seemed like one large cemetery. But when the
conversation shifted to the newspaper *Hatzvi* and
the Ben-Yehudah dictionary, he became bored and
slipped out of the house. It was an autumn evening. There was a breeze in the air which carried a
whiff of the freshly ploughed fields. He could hear
children shouting in the distance, and he followed
the sound.

"I am Ben-Zion Ben-Yehudah from Jerusalem,"
he said, introducing himself.

"Your father is Ben-Yehudah?" they asked.
Their voices did not contain the note of sneering
which he was accustomed to hearing from boys his
age in Jerusalem. On the contrary, their voices were
full of admiration and even envy. They were jealous
of him for being the son of the famous Ben-
Yehudah.

"Want to join us, Ben-Zion?" they asked. "We

are going to the barn. Do you think your folks will let you come along?"

Ben-Zion clambered over the highest bundle of straw and rolled down, shouting gleefully with the other children. It was so good here, in this quiet village, it was so peaceful and warm and friendly. Nobody laughed at him for speaking Hebrew. They were all his friends.

When the sound of singing was heard, the children picked themselves up and cleaned the straw from their clothes. "Come along," they told Ben-Zion. "They've started singing and dancing. They're really enjoying themselves over there. Let's go and join them."

Ben Zion would have loved to stay in the village a little longer and play with his new friends. But Ben-Yehudah was in a hurry to be off.

"I am afraid we have to cut our trip short this time. There is a great deal of work waiting for me in Jerusalem. Only yesterday did I begin to understand just how important my dictionary really is. I must provide words for the people who wish to speak Hebrew. This is no time for journeys and sightseeing. Time is short and there is much to be done."

"But Abba," said Ben-Zion angrily, "you promised we would go to so many places."

"Some other time, my son," said Eliezer. Then he realized how badly upset and disappointed the boy was. "Do you know what?" he said. "Tomorrow the train will leave Jaffa on its first journey to Jerusalem. Would you like to go home by train?"

Ben-Zion's eyes shone. To travel by train! For that he was quite willing to forgo the rest of the journey.

When they reached Jaffa, Chemdah, who was accustomed to European trains, soon saw that this train was only an old steam engine with three small carriages. To her it seemed more like a toy than a train. But Ben-Zion, who had only seen pictures of trains, was thrilled and excited.

"Does the train really travel by itself, without horses? You mean to say that we can actually reach Jerusalem this evening by train? So quickly?"

They climbed up the stairs. The carriages moved—a slight shifting movement—and the train was on its way.

"It's going so fast!" exclaimed Ben-Zion, standing at the window with the wind blowing through his hair.

"What's this? What happened? Why has the train stopped?" cried Ben-Zion when the train halted half an hour later.

When they looked out the window they saw a strange sight. Arab horsemen were standing on the rails with their horses and donkeys and would not move. They were shouting and gesticulating and screwing up their faces in fury.

"What do they want?" asked Chemdah. "Why are they so angry?"

Eliezer listened to what was being said, and explained. "They claim that the 'horseless carriage'— as they call the train—is the devil's work; that it is a demon running with its smoke blowing. They are not prepared to let this demon pass close to their village. They are afraid it is evil. I had better go down and explain it to them."

Eliezer spent a long time with the excited Arabs. Finally the Arabs agreed to get off the rails and let the train continue its journey.

"It is not easy to switch over from the age of the camel to a modern train," sighed Eliezer, wiping his forehead tiredly, as he climbed back to his carriage.

The engine moved on through the mountains. Ben-Zion was very impressed by its strength, which enabled it to carry such a load and did not make it necessary for anyone to get off and push it uphill.

"Why do they stop every other minute?" he asked his father. "Whenever anybody stands up on the rails and signals to them, the engine driver stops to pick him up. I can't stand it."

"This doesn't happen on most trains," Chemdah explained. "Real trains have proper stations and regular timetables. Our train must be a particularly good one, because it tries to satisfy everybody."

"The day will come, Chemdah dear," said Eliezer, "when we, too, shall have fast trains, just as they do in Moscow. One day the journey from Jaffa to Jerusalem will take only a few hours. By that time Jerusalem will be a proper city with factories, fine shops, and busy streets. Other large towns will also spring up in this country, and there will be many villages all over. One day this desert will become a fertile land—the land of the Jews. They will return from everywhere to their homeland. They will come back to the Hebrew language from seventy different tongues."

Ben-Zion looked at his father. Suddenly he appeared to him like a prophet of old, as he stood there with his reddish pointed beard and his eyes glittering with the fervor of his belief.

"The day will come . . .the day will come . . . the day will come . . ." sang the wheels of the train.

The Little Heroes of Kfar Tabor

an Israeli folktale,
translated by
Azriel Eisenberg and Leah Ain Globe

*Before Israel was established as a Jewish state
in 1948, the Turkish government ruled the land.
Many rules and regulations made the lives of the
settlers difficult.*

*Turkish soldiers wanted to destroy the new
building in Kfar Tabor. Here's how the children
saved their school.*

At the foot of Mt. Tabor in the Galilee there is
a small settlement by the name of Kfar Tabor.
Soon after it was established, its inhabitants decided to build a large and beautiful school.

The Turks ruled the land of Israel in those
days. They refused to give the Jews permission to
put up any kind of structure. The Turks were
afraid that if they allowed them to build houses,
many Jews would come to Israel to live, and they
would establish a government of Israel. However,
the Turks had a law that if a building was already
up and it had a roof, no one was permitted to
demolish it.

41

The Jews of the settlement decided to build a school in a hurry and put a roof on it before the authorities would find out. This happened in the summer time during the long vacation. The children went out with their fathers to the fields and, except for the hammering of builders, all was quiet in the settlement. The walls of the new school went up higher and higher each day and soon the roof would go up.

On the day that the walls were finished, several children came running up to the builders to tell them that they had seen Turkish soldiers marching toward the settlement. The workers knew what that meant. The building would be razed and they would be thrown into prison. The settlement leader told them to stop work immediately, and when the soldiers arrived the men were nowhere to be found, for they had taken refuge in nearby houses.

The Turkish commander glanced at the partly finished building and ordered: "Demolish the house! Leave no stone unturned!"

The children of Kfar Tabor knew why the soldiers had come and they said to each other, "We will not let them tear down our school!"

They rushed over with lightning speed, climbed the walls from all sides, covering the top like a living crown. The soldiers tried to get the children down, but the youngsters clung to the stones of the walls.

"Get down from those walls!" the commander shouted, stamping his foot.

"This is our school," the children answered.

"We are going to study here. We will protect it with all our might. We won't get off until you leave the settlement!"

"If you don't come down," growled the commander, "we'll drag you down and throw you into prison."

"No matter what you do, we won't come down."

The children sat on the walls all day long. When night fell, and the commander saw that the children wouldn't move, he turned to his soldiers and said, "Let's go! We'll come back before sunrise and tear it down."

As soon as the soldiers left, the head of the Kfar Tabor settlement sent messages to all the neighboring settlements to come quickly so that they might help them cover the building with a roof.

All night long the men from Kfar Tabor worked together with their neighbors. They hammered and sawed and nailed. They did not let sleep overtake them. When dawn broke there was a roof on their school building!

Just then the soldiers arrived with sledge hammers, axes, and crowbars, prepared to throw down the walls of the school. They were very angry when they saw the roof up, but they couldn't do a thing.

The school building is standing in Kfar Tabor to this day. And now, the children's children of those little heroes study there.

In America,
the Golden Land

Waiting for Mama

by Marietta Moskin

In Russia, Jewish people lived in fear of the czar and his soldiers. Papa wanted to start a new life of freedom in America, so he came here with Becky and her older sister and brother. Mama had to stay behind with baby Leah until Leah was cured of an eye disease.

They all worked hard and saved money to bring Mama and Leah to New York. Becky could hardly wait for their arrival, especially since she was planning a wonderful surprise for Mama.

"Only two weeks," Rachel sighed, making her needle flash as fast as she could. "How will I ever finish?"

Two whole weeks, Becky thought. How can I ever wait that long? Two weeks will never go by.

But even for Becky the days passed quickly. There was so much to do.

She watched Mama's coat grow bit by bit under Rachel's clever fingers. One day there were only pieces of cloth. Then they took shape: first

one sleeve. Then the other. A collar; pockets; but-
tonholes. How grand Mama would look walking
down the block in that coat! All the neighbors
would stop and stare after her.

"That's Becky's mother," they would whisper.
"That fine lady is Becky's Mama from Russia."

Will Mama like her new home? Becky wondered. She wasn't sure. She remembered how it
had looked to her when she first came. She remembered the dirty walls, the cold, sour smells in the
halls, the ugly spots on the floors. The rooms were
much cozier now. The window was hung with
curtains. They had a rug on the floor. But the stairs
and the halls were still dirty and dark, and you
never could escape the mingling odors of cabbage
cooking and rancid oil and stale air. Becky hardly
noticed the smells anymore. After two years you
got used to such things. But would Mama mind?
Mama had never lived in a house crowded with so
many strangers.

And Mama was used to a garden. Here there
was only a fire escape. And the five flights of stairs
were narrow and steep when you had to carry out
the trash and ashes.

Mama will like the water tap in the hall, Becky
decided. In Senjiki you had to go outside to the
pump. That was hard work. Here you only needed
to turn on a tap. And the toilet was right indoors in
the hall one flight down. You didn't have to go
outdoors in bad weather.

"Mama will be happy because she'll be with

us," Papa said. "Life in America is hard but free. We need not be afraid of the czar's soldiers."

And Mama will have a fine coat, Becky thought. As nice a coat as any you'd find in the stores on Canal Street.

Becky herself sewed on the six buttons. It took a long time. Mama's buttons must be secure, Becky thought.

Then she helped Rachel hide the coat. It was a surprise even for Papa.

And then the big day arrived. It was time to go and meet Mama and baby Leah. Papa dressed up in his bowler hat. Rachel and Jake and Becky wore their best clothes.

"Dress warmly. It's cold outside," Papa warned. "The first real autumn weather."

Rachel and Becky looked at each other. "Mama's coat," they whispered—almost at the same time.

Rachel ran to get the coat from its hiding place. She folded it neatly and carried it over her arm. Papa didn't even notice. He was too busy trying to remember how to get to the dock.

"We must take the horsecar to the ferry landing," he told them.

On Broadway, Becky clung to Rachel's hand. So much traffic! Milk wagons, ice wagons, delivery trucks, fast carriages with sleek horses. . . . How could you ever cross a busy street like that? In their own neighborhood the streets were crowded, too—but traffic could never move fast because the streets were narrow and twisting, and they were always clogged with pushcarts and with shoppers walking in the middle of the road.

Becky had hardly ever been this far out of her own neighborhood. It was like seeing a different city.

"Is this the right horsecar?" Papa wondered. He didn't know how to ask. The car conductor would not speak Russian. This was never a problem in their own neighborhood. On Hester Street and Orchard Street and in the place where he worked, everybody spoke either Russian or Polish or Yiddish or a mixture of all three. Nobody ever had to worry about speaking proper English. But now they were in a different part of town. The real American part.

"I will ask," Becky said. "I can ask in English."

"So can I . . ." Jake started, but when he saw Becky's eager face, he swallowed back his words.

"Yes, Becky, you ask," he said, grinning at Rachel. "Show us how well you can speak."

On the ferry ride to Ellis Island Becky sat very still. She still didn't like boats and ships. And she remembered how she had hated the immigration station.

"Where do we go now?" Papa wondered when they were off the ferry.

"This sign says 'Visitors,' " Becky said. "I guess that's us." In the big arrival hall there were many people.

"Are these the passengers from Mama's ship?" Papa asked.

"I'll ask the guard," Becky said—and she did.

"What would we do without Becky?" Papa said, winking at Jake. "Isn't it lucky that she learned English so well. That can be your gift to Mama, Becky. That's what you did while we earned money to bring her over."

Becky squeezed Rachel's hand. She smiled a secret smile. Papa still didn't know about her real present for Mama!

She looked at the crowd in the room. Will we recognize Mama? she wondered. Will she recognize us? I have changed in two years. I've lost my baby teeth in the front. My hair is longer and not as curly as it was. And I've grown a lot taller.

Becky looked and looked. There were too many people. All the faces were blurring together. Then she saw something green. A familiar green shawl.

"Mama, Mama," Becky cried.

Mama carried a big sack over her shoulder. Leah was next to her. She wasn't a baby anymore. She walked, holding onto Mama's skirt.

And then Becky was in Mama's arms, and everybody was crying.

On the ferry, they all clustered around Mama.

"Look, over there, that's America," Papa said.

"Thank God," Mama said, wiping a tear from her eyes.

Becky watched Mama standing by the railing, her skirt billowing in the cool harbor breeze. She saw how Mama shivered and pulled her shawl closer around her shoulders.

"Look, Rachel," she whispered. "Mama is cold."

"The coat!" Rachel cried. She rushed over to Mama. "Here, Mama—put this on now. It's a gift— my gift and Becky's. Put it on, Mama, it will keep you warm."

And now Mama's tears really flowed as she pulled on her coat and hugged Rachel and Becky in turn.

"Such a beautiful coat—so soft—so warm. . . ." Mama hardly could get the words out between laughing and crying. She hugged the coat to herself, stroking the soft wool.

Afterward Becky never remembered the ferry ride back to the city because they were all so busy talking about the coat. Rachel and Becky told about working secretly to earn extra money and how Becky had earned and chosen the buttons herself. Papa kept shaking his head, but Becky knew he wasn't really angry, because of the way he smiled to himself.

Later, when they boarded the horsecar going home, it was once again Becky who asked directions. She could see Mama looking at her in surprise.

"My little Becky," Mama said. "Chattering away in English. I can't believe what I hear!"

Becky felt as if she would burst with pride. She held tight to Mama's hand, while Rachel held Leah.

Jake carried Mama's big bundle. He was too old to hold onto Mama as Becky did, but his eyes never left her face.

Papa told Mama how hard they all had worked to earn money to bring her over.

"And Becky went to school," Papa said. "Besides earning money for buttons, she studied hard. She learned to read and write. She learned to speak English, as you can see. Becky will be your guide. Becky can be your helper."

Mama hugged Becky. "What wonderful children I have," she said. "Now I need not worry about New York anymore. Now I don't have to be afraid because I can't speak the language. I have an American daughter."

Becky's face glowed with surprise when she heard Mama's words.

Mama is right, I *am* an American girl, she thought. Nearly as American as my teacher, Miss Harris. And I didn't even know it.

And Becky snuggled as close against Mama as she possibly could.

Ben Goes Into Business
by Marilyn Hirsh

*With only ten cents, what could Ben possibly
do for his family? He had help from a sea monster,
Bel Traffio the Magnificent, a crying child, pancakes on a high wire, and more. . . .*

In New York City, quite a while ago, there
lived a rather large family whose oldest son was
called Ben.

Ben remembered the old country and the
village where the family had lived before they
came to America. His father, Isaac, had been the
greatest Hebrew scholar for miles around. Everyone went to him for advice. But then war came and
soldiers with guns. One dark night the family left
their village. Finally they came to the harbor and
got on a big boat to come to America with hundreds of other people.

In America Ben's father could not make a
living as a scholar. There were already many,
many scholars in the big city. So he took a job that
he could learn in a hurry. He became a pants

presser, though his mind still thought great thoughts. He didn't make much money at all.

So the family was very poor. Ben worried a lot. He wanted to help earn more money.

One day a friend of Ben's told him about a big park on the ocean called Coney Island. He said it was over the bridge and far away. Many rich people went there to play games and ride on rides. They went swimming and sunned themselves on the beach and strolled along the boardwalk in their fine clothes.

Ben could hardly imagine such splendors.

Best of all, his friend told him, a smart boy could make money selling these rich people all-day suckers.

"But," Ben's friend said, "you'll need ten cents to start with. There's a man in a booth near the sea monster who will sell you ten suckers for ten cents."

But where to get that first ten cents? Ben decided to ask his mother if she would lend him the money. He knew ten cents would buy enough potatoes for a whole meal for the whole family.

How could he ask his mother to part with so much money? How could he be sure that he would be able to sell his suckers and pay her back?

"What's the matter, Benjy? You look worried," his mother said.

So Ben told her the whole plan. "If I sell ten suckers at two cents apiece, I would have twenty cents. With the twenty cents I could get twenty suckers and if I sold them all, I'd have forty cents. Then I could pay back the ten cents and make you a present of thirty cents!"

"Not so fast, Benjy," his mother said. But she gave him the ten cents.

On Sunday morning while the rest of the family was asleep, Ben got up. It was still dark. Soon his mother was up, too. She made him warm cereal.

"If business is so good that you stay all day," his mother said, "buy yourself lunch from your profits." She stuffed an apple into his pocket.

The streets were almost empty in the half light of dawn. As Ben crossed the Brooklyn Bridge, a tugboat tooted and the sun came up. "What a day!" he said to himself as he waved to the tugboat captain.

After much more walking, he found the booth near the sea monster. And sure enough there was a man selling all-day suckers.

Ben bought ten.

"Now, I'm really in business!" he said to himself.

Suddenly he was very hungry. He pulled out his apple and took a bite even though he meant to save it for lunch.

He went right down to the beach, far from the other boys who were selling things. "All-day suckers only two cents!" he shouted.

Ben was so excited to be in business that he walked right into the ocean—shoes and all!

Whenever he heard a child crying he would run up and say to the mother, "All-day sucker, Madam? It will keep your little boy smiling all day long!"

He sold his ten suckers. With the twenty cents, he bought twenty more. "You sold out fast for your first day," said the vendor.

After about an hour of brisk selling, Ben's feet were dragging. He decided to rest near a tall tower because there was a circus show going on. The tightrope act was so daring that he just sat there and forgot all about business.

On a high thin wire, Bel Traffio the Magnificent walked on his hands, did splits, and turned a somersault in the air. He juggled plates without dropping any, while Ben held his breath.

For the grand finale of his act, Bel Traffio's beautiful assistant, in pink tights and a tiny fluffy skirt, handed him something that looked like a stove.

It was a stove! As Ben watched in amazement, Bel Traffio the Magnificent lit the stove. He then stirred something in a bowl and soon was busy making pancakes. Ben got a crick in his neck staring up and watching him.

Bel Traffio the Magnificent flipped the pancakes high in the air and caught them on a plate. Ben cheered and so did the crowd. But the sight of the pancakes made Ben realize that he was starving.

"It's a long time since I ate the apple," Ben thought.

All around him people were eating. "Except me," he said to himself.

He counted his money. He had twenty-eight cents. He could easily buy something to eat. Still he hated to spend any of it. "I worked too hard to earn it," he decided.

All of a sudden Ben had an idea. He raced to Bel Traffio's tent. "Mr. Traffio," he called as loudly as he dared.

Bel Traffio appeared with his assistant. The great tightrope walker looked very fierce close up. But his assistant smiled at Ben.

In a small voice, Ben said, "I just came to tell you that I think your act is the best of all, but . . ."

"But what?" roared Bel Traffio the Magnificent.

"Well," said Ben in an even smaller voice. "There's just one thing wrong." He rushed on. "People don't believe that you are making real pancakes all the way up there!"

"They don't?" bellowed Bel Traffio the Magnificent. "And what do you propose to do about it?"

"If you will flip them down to me, I'll eat them. Then people will know they're real."

"Not a bad idea," said the friendly assistant.

"We'll try you out at the two o'clock show," Bel Traffio the Magnificent said, as he strode behind the curtain.

"I'll be there," said Ben.

By two o'clock Ben had sold his last all-day

sucker. He was so hungry that he could hardly wait to play his part in the tightrope walker's act.

When the pancakes started falling, Ben caught them and gobbled them as fast as he could.

The people laughed and clapped for Ben and for Bel Traffio the Magnificent.

At the end of the act, the lovely lady passed the hat. She got more coins than ever before. "Here's twenty cents for you, Ben," she said. "You earned it."

Bel Traffio appeared. He didn't seem quite as fierce as before. "Can you come and eat my pancakes next Sunday?" he asked.

"I can come every Sunday," said Ben.

"Where do you live, Ben?" asked the lady, who was Mrs. Bel Traffio the Magnificent.

"Just over the Brooklyn Bridge," said Ben.

"Well, we're going that way, too," she said, "so a ride comes with the job."

When Ben reached his street, sitting on the tailgate of Bel Traffio's magnificent wagon, all the kids on his block and a lot of the grownups, too, crowded around asking a million questions.

"I'll tell you about it later," said Ben grandly and waved goodbye to the Bel Traffios.

Ben dashed up the stairs to his apartment and flung open the door. He was so out of breath that he couldn't say a word. Silently he pressed sixty cents into his mother's hand.

While she slowly counted out the pennies and

the other coins, Ben's brothers and sisters and his father gathered around.

"In the new country," his father said, "our firstborn is already a candy merchant at ten years old."

"And I got a job too," said Ben.

"Don't tell anymore until I come back," said Ben's mother, putting on her shawl. "I'm going to the butcher to get a chicken. Tonight we'll have a feast!"

P'Idyon Ha-Ben

by Sydney Taylor

Charlie was looking forward to a ceremony to celebrate the birth of his new cousin. Uncle Hyman had invited everyone, including their neighbors who weren't Jewish.

Charlie got a bit mixed up about the P'Idyon Ha-Ben—*he was waiting to see "Benny the pigeon."*

Even today, a boy baby has a circumcision, a brit, *when he is eight days old. In addition, a firstborn boy has a* P'Idyon Ha-Ben *celebration when he is one month old.*

Early one morning there was a banging on the kitchen door. "That could only be Uncle Hyman," Mama said. "He's the one that always bangs—Oh, my, do you suppose the baby has come? Come in," she called out.

The door opened, and Uncle Hyman swaggered in. "It's a boy!" he shouted. "My Lena's had a boy!" He danced around the room and snapped his suspenders. His small blue eyes and jolly round face were shining with happiness.

"Oh, Hyman, I'm so happy for you!" Mama cried, and the children gathered around, patting him on the back and dancing with him.

Papa grabbed Uncle Hyman by the shoulder. "A firstborn and a son! That's really something to celebrate!"

"Yes!" declared Uncle Hyman. "My son will have the finest *P'Idyon Ha-Ben* a child could ever have! Everybody's invited—I mean everybody!" His eyes came to rest on Grace's astonished face. "And you too, young lady," he said, pointing at her. He dashed for the door. "I gotta go! I got a million things to attend to."

"Good-by, Hyman. Tell Lena we wish her all the best," Mama called after him.

Grace turned to Ella, "It's nice of your uncle to invite me, but what's he talking about?"

Ella laughed. "In Jewish families when the first child is a son, they have a ceremony which is called *P'Idyon Ha-Ben*. That means redemption of the son. It takes place one month after the child is born. It's a sort of party, really. You'll enjoy it."

A month seemed a long way off, but it was surprising how quickly the time passed. For days before, Mama had gone to Lena's house to help with the preparations. It was hard to tell who was more excited, Mama or Lena. "You'd think it was a *P'Idyon Ha-Ben* of her own," Papa teased.

When the family and Grace arrived on the party day, they found Lena's apartment already crowded with guests. Friends, neighbors, and relatives milled about in all their finery, glad to be together on such a joyous occasion.

Uncle Hyman and Aunt Lena were off in a corner, chatting with Mrs. Shiner. Catching sight of the family, all three pushed their way toward them. Lena, plumper and more rosy-cheeked than ever, kissed them heartily. "My beautiful nieces and my favorite nephew!"

"May we see the baby, Lena?" Gertie asked.

"Why not?"

They filed into the bedroom and tiptoed over to the crib. "Oh, how sweet!" "Isn't he cunning!" they whispered. "Look, Charlie, look at the tiny little baby."

Charlie stared at the infant. "It's like a doll."

The baby stirred and stretched his little arms over his head. His little face puckered. He yawned—a big, big yawn. "Yes, Charlie," Charlotte said, "it's a live doll!"

Uncle Hyman came in to remind them that it was time for the ceremony.

Charlie tugged at Mama's skirt. "Now can I see the pigeon?" he asked loudly.

They all stopped to listen to Charlie's strange request. "Pigeon," Mama repeated, puzzled. "What pigeon?"

Charlie explained patiently. "You said we were going to a party and there's a pigeon and his name is Ben. I don't see no pigeon."

"Pigeon Ben! It does sound like it!" Henny squealed with laughter. "He means the *P'Idyon*

Ha-Ben. He expected to see a real live pigeon!"

Why was everyone laughing so hard, wondered Charlie. "I wanna see Benny the pigeon!" he insisted.

Papa swept him up in his arms. "Charlie, what you're going to see is even better—like a little play. Come, and I'll explain it all to you while we're watching." He smiled at Grace. "And to you too, Grace."

In the parlor, the company had already arranged themselves in a wide circle. A tall, thin man dressed in a frock coat stepped forward. "That's the Cohan," Papa told Grace. "A Cohan is descended from the tribe of Aaron. Only such a one is allowed to perform this ceremony. In ancient times, the oldest son was required to serve in the Temple. If one wanted to release his child from this service, he had to pay for it. Today the Cohan will act like the High Priest in the Temple of old."

The room grew quiet. Presently Uncle Hyman appeared from the bedroom. On a cushion in his arms lay the baby, dressed in an exquisitely embroidered white dress. Solemnly he walked to the Cohan and offered the child up to him. He began to recite in Hebrew. Grace turned to Papa inquiringly. In a low whisper, Papa translated. "This, my firstborn, is the firstborn of his mother. . ."

The Cohan took the child from his father. "Which do you prefer," he asked, "to give me thy firstborn for God's service . . . or to redeem him for five shekels which you are by law required to give?"

Charlie pulled on Papa's hand. "Papa, why is that man taking the baby from Uncle Hyman?"

"Don't worry, Charlie. Uncle Hyman'll get him back."

Uncle Hyman held up five silver dollars and answered the Cohan. "I prefer to redeem my son. Here is the value . . . which I am by law obliged to pay."

The Cohan accepted the money and returned the child to Uncle Hyman. Holding the coins over the infant's head, the Cohan proclaimed: "*This* is an exchange of *that*. . . May it be the will of God that . . . this child may be spared to enter the study of the law, the state of marriage, and the practice of good deeds. Amen!"

Placing his hands upon the baby's head, he blessed the little one: "The Lord shall guard thee against all evil . . . Amen!"

"Amen!" answered the guests. "May you have much joy and honor from him!" They crowded around, ohing and ahing over the baby and showering congratulations on the parents.

As the guests circled about, Uncle Hyman started shooing them toward the dining room. "Let's go to the table! Let's go to the table!" he coaxed.

They didn't need much urging. The sight of the table piled high with delicious-looking food whetted everyone's appetite. Uncle Hyman scurried around filling glasses with schnapps or wine.

Everyone ate heartily—laughing and singing and telling stories in between. They complimented Lena on her excellent cooking, and her rosy face blushed even rosier with pleasure. Everybody was having a fine time.

It was late when at last the party began to break up. Tired and happy, the family groups started to leave. "May we always come together on joyous occasions," was the parting wish as they fondly embraced one another.

"Girls," Lena whispered as she put her arms around Ella and Grace, "Being married and having a baby is the most wonderful thing in the world. *Merchum* by you!" (May it happen to you.) For answer, Ella kissed Aunt Lena.

"Thank you so much for letting me come," Grace said. "I really enjoyed it."

"I'm glad," Uncle Hyman beamed. "Come again. Any time you like."

Charlie was so tired that Papa had to carry him all the way home. They were just entering the house when the little boy suddenly raised his head. "Papa," he asked, "does the Cohan keep all the pigeon money for himself?"

"Oh, no, Charlie," replied Papa. "The *P'Idyon Ha-Ben* money goes to charity."

In the State of Israel

The House in the Tree
by Molly Cone

Modern Israel has lots of cactus plants and olive trees, buses and tractors, soldier girls and taxi men—but very little wood. Yaacov wants to build a tree house like the one he left at home in America. How will he ever find some wood?

In his aunt's house, everybody talked at once. Everybody asked questions, and everybody answered. Everybody but Yaacov.

He sat and stared out into the thick green branches of an olive tree.

Here everybody called him *Yaacov* instead of Jacob. Even his father and mother called him Yaacov since they had come to Israel. It was the way to say his name in Hebrew.

"Yaacov!" said his father. "Listen!"

"Just like his grandfather!" said Yaacov's mother. "Sits without ears!"

Yaacov turned his head to listen. But what he listened to was the whispering of the olive leaves.

"For Yaacov, everything is new," said his aunt.

His older cousin Izik grinned at him. Izik was
a *sabra*. All children born in Israel were called
sabras after the cactus plant that grew everywhere
in the land. The cactus fruit was tough and prickly
on the outside. But the inside tasted sweet.

Half of everything that was Izik's was now
Yaacov's. Half his table, half his cupboard, half his
bed. Half this house would be Yaacov's house all
the year his family stayed in Israel.

"In America, Yaacov learned to say all the
prayers in Hebrew," said Yaacov's mother proudly.

"But you have to live in Israel to learn what the
words really mean," said his aunt softly.

Yaacov gazed at the olive tree. He saw thick
wide limbs and a place for a floor. He saw a green-
branched ceiling and space for a door.

"I think I will build a tree house," he said.

"A house in a tree?" His aunt seemed surprised.

Yaacov nodded. That's what he meant. A
house in a tree. Like the one he had left in the
empty lot back home.

Everybody laughed. Izik's was the loudest.

But Yaacov saw nothing to laugh about.

"In that tree," he said.

They all looked at the tree. It stood outside
their house of stone. It was an old tree. It might
have been the same tree King David once sat
under, it was so old.

In Israel many things were very old—as old as
the land, the rocks, and the hills. And many things

were very new—as new as the farms, the forests, and the flag.

"It is a land of miracles!" Izik's mother was always saying. As if miracles still grew from the ancient ground like the olive trees.

"You've got to have *wood* to build a house in a tree," Izik said.

"I'll find some," said Yaacov.

Their laughter followed him across the stony yard, past the low wall down the bare road.

"Don't go far!" his mother called after him.

He went past the store where his aunt bought dried peas and sesame seeds and orange drink.

He went past the stand where Izik and his friends bought *felafel* and *pita*. The pita was round and flat and looked like a pancake. Inside was the spicy hot ball of mashed chickpeas called a felafel. An Israeli ate felafel and pita almost as often as an American ate a hamburger in a bun.

A bus came around the bend of the hill. On its side was D A N.

"Do you know where I can find some wood?" Yaacov shouted as the bus went slowly by.

But the driver only waved his hand.

Two soldier girls came walking by. Yaacov ran along beside them.

"Do you know where I can find some wood?"

One girl shrugged, pushed out her lip, and turned the palms of her hands up.

"I know where there's plenty of wood," the other said.

"Where?" shouted Yaacov.

"Over there." She waved toward the hilltop. "We just planted a whole forest up there!"

Yaacov looked at the new forest on the hillside. The tallest tree was as high as his knee. He watched the soldier girls walk away.

A young man came riding along on a tractor. He wore shorts and sandals. A round faded hat was tipped over his eyes, kibbutz-style.

A farm that was a kibbutz was a very special kind of farm in Israel. Many, many families lived together on each kibbutz like one large family. Everyone shared the work to be done. Everything on the kibbutz belonged to everybody equally. Kibbutz farmers were very important to the little country of Israel. They were making the old land new again.

"Wood?" the man yelled down. "It's against the law to cut down a tree in Israel! Nothing much of anything grew here until we came and planted. Nothing but rocks!"

Yaacov stood at the side of the road and watched the tractor disappear.

A big black taxi had stopped in the middle of the road. The driver got out, opened the hood, and looked in.

A cloud of steam blew out. The man jumped back and laughed.

"Do you think I can find some wood anywhere around here?"

"Why not?" said the taxi man. "They say miracles happen every day in Israel."

Yaacov blinked.

"Ask anyone. Everyone has a miracle to tell you. It's a miracle we Jews are here!"

Yaacov watched him slam down the hood of his car and wipe his hands on a rag.

"Before I came to Israel, where did I live?"

"Where?" asked Yaacov.

"Nowhere," said the man who drove the taxi. "In the country where I was born and where I grew up, there came a leader who said: '*Jews! This is not your home.*' And he took away my house and he took away all the things I loved. No place was my home anymore."

The man stood up straight and took a deep breath.

"*In Israel no one can say to me: 'This is not your home.*'

"Two thousand years we waited and we dreamed. And finally we learned—'If you will it, it's no dream.'"

He winked at Yaacov. "Learning always takes time," he said. And he got back into his car.

"But I can't wait two thousand years!" Yaacov ran after him to shout.

"What's the matter?" said his father when Yaacov sat down at the breakfast table.

"Nothing," he said.

"What's the matter?" said his mother when Yaacov didn't go out to play.

"In Israel, everyone has problems," his aunt said. "So why shouldn't Yaacov have one too? If you didn't have problems, you wouldn't have miracles!" She smiled at Yaacov. "So now you are a real Israeli."

Yaacov tried to laugh. He didn't believe in miracles.

He helped Izik weed the carrots. "*Todah rabah*," said Izik. Half of Izik's chores were Yaacov's too.

"In Israel everybody helps," his aunt said. "Everything counts."

She held up an apple. "From the inside we make sauce or juice. From the outside, jam."

"You could make your tree house out of an old blanket," his mother said.

Yaacov shook his head.

"You could use rope to make a hammock," said his father.

"Or weave reeds into a basket like the one that held the baby Moses," his aunt said.

"You have to have wood to build a house in a tree," Yaacov said.

And no one laughed.

Izik said loudly, "We have more work to do! We have to go to the Post Office today."

Yaacov went to the Post Office to help Izik. He stood around while Izik filled out slips. He stared at the people going in and out.

If you will it, it's no dream.

"Here it is!" Izik said.

Yaacov turned around.

Izik was standing next to something. It was very large.

"Books," said Izik.

Yaacov opened his eyes wide. "Wood!" he cried.

"Oh," said Izik. Then he opened his mouth and closed it again. He put his hand on the box.

"It's half yours," he said carefully.

Yaacov held his breath. "Which half?"

"The books inside are mine," Izik said.

Yaacov looked at the crate and saw the house in the tree. He saw a floor of boards—wide as a floor should be.

"And the wood outside is mine!"

Izik grinned at him. "When you live in Israel, you have to believe in miracles," he said.

Yaacov laughed. Loud as you please. The way all Israelis laugh. "I know it," he said.

Miriam Lives in a Kibbutz
by Cordelia Edwardson

When Miriam arrived in Israel from Morocco, everything seemed new and strange. She didn't like living in a kibbutz. She didn't want to sleep in the children's house. She didn't want so many brothers and sisters all at once.

Her new friend Daniel knew just what to do.

The first time anyone said "*Shalom!*" to Miriam was when she arrived in Israel with her mother and father. She came in an airplane from Morocco.

"Now we are at home," Miriam's father said to her. "Your great-great-great—I can't count far enough back, but about two thousand years ago all our family and all other Jews lived here in Israel. Then there was a war and nearly all the Jews were driven out of Israel. For two thousand years they had to live in other countries, but they could never forget Israel. Now many Jews from all parts of the world have returned to Israel, and we, too, are here." Miriam understood that her father and mother were glad.

She remembered the feast they had celebrated in Morocco every year at Passover time. "Next year in Israel," they had all said to each other when the feast ended. Now it had come true.

When Miriam reached the kibbutz where they were all to live she was not at all pleased. She was angry because she was not allowed to live with her mother and father. Like all the other children in the kibbutz, she was to live in the children's own house. There, all the children slept, ate and played together.

Miriam sat silent and angry at the corner of the table and ate her food, and she did not answer the other children when they asked what it was like to fly in an airplane.

When one of the women at the children's house started to read a good-night story, Miriam did not want to listen, although she was usually very fond of stories. All she wanted was to go home to her mother and father. When her mother came to tuck her into bed, Miriam asked, "Can't you stay, just for tonight?"

Her mother shook her head, "Not tonight. But soon we will have a house of our own in the kibbutz and we can all be together on Saturdays. The rest of the week we will have to work, and you will stay in the children's house with your new friends."

Miriam did not think this was a very good idea

and she wept a long time before she fell asleep.

The next day, the women wanted Miriam to play with the other children, but she would not join in their games. She was still very unhappy and sulky. In Morocco she had never had any playmates, and she had always wanted brothers and sisters. "But I don't want so many, and not all at once—and not without Mother and Father," she thought.

Miriam knew that if she joined in the games, everyone would think that she was beginning to like living in the children's house. But she would never do that, and she made up her mind to find her mother and tell her so.

Miriam had a hard time finding her mother in the big kitchen where the women were fixing lunch. All the grownups in the kibbutz eat together in a large canteen, and the women take turns cooking for the others. "Run along and play with the other children," her mother said. "Soon five hundred hungry people will come in asking for food, and I haven't time to talk to you now."

Miriam was even angrier. She'd always helped her mother in the kitchen in Morocco, and now her mother didn't even have time to talk to her. But perhaps her father would have time.

Father was driving a tractor in a field. He hugged Miriam and tried to comfort her. But he could not promise that everything would be the

same as it had been in Morocco. "You must understand," he said, "that we all have to work hard to
make a really fine kibbutz."

"Kibbutz, kibbutz—that's all they think
about—but I don't care about it at all," thought
Miriam, and she sat down and screamed as hard as
she could.

Suddenly she caught sight of a boy sitting and
laughing at her. But he had a pleasant laugh. "Hi,"
he said. "My name is Daniel. Why don't you stop
crying and come play with me? You may borrow
my flashlight while I climb this tree." No one had
ever been allowed to borrow it before, for Daniel
was afraid the batteries would run down.

"I live in that house over there," said Daniel.
"When Mother and Father have finished work and
eaten you can come and see us. Then I can go
with you to the children's house where we are to
sleep."

"How funny," thought Miriam. "He seems
to like sleeping in the children's house," and she
asked Daniel if he would read an extra story for
her that night.

"Of course I will," said Daniel. "I can read a
story for you now, too." They went off together to
the library where there were books all the way up
to the ceiling. Daniel could read very well.

"But," thought Miriam, "he is eight, and I am
only five."

"Let's go and see my mother now," said Daniel.
"She works in the dress store." Daniel's mother was

not there just then, but Daniel found a lovely white blouse with a border of red and blue flowers. He asked Miriam if she would like to try it on.

"Of course I would. But we shall never be able to afford it," she sighed.

"Oh, but you will," said Daniel. "The best thing about a kibbutz is that we can all afford as much as one other. When we sell our oranges and apples and all the other things that we make in the kibbutz, we share the money equally. That's the right thing to do, because everyone has helped."

So Miriam tried on the blouse.

"Come with me to see my grandfather," said Daniel. Grandfather worked in a juice factory. He showed Miriam all the boxes full of orange juice and apple juice ready to be sent away.

"What hard work it must be to press all those oranges and apples to make juice," said Miriam.

"They are pressed in machines," Daniel explained, "and my father looks after the machines."

"And my father makes the apple trees and the orange trees grow," said Miriam. She was not quite sure whether that was true, but she said it anyway.

Daniel had saved to the last the best thing in the kibbutz—the big new swimming pool.

"We can thank the apples for this," he said. "We sold so much apple juice that we could afford to build this swimming pool. We had only a shower before."

Daniel told Miriam that he had a secret to tell her. He whispered in her ear, but when she said

that she could not hear what he said he laughed at
her. "I have a secret, I have a secret, which I won't
tell you, which I won't tell you," he sang.

After that, Miriam could think of nothing else
but the secret.

Later, the children changed for the Sabbath.
Miriam put on the fine blouse she had wished for,
and then she learned the secret. She was to be
"Queen of the Sabbath." The other children had
chosen her. The Queen of the Sabbath lights the
Sabbath candles, which is a great honor.

Miriam did not want anyone but Daniel to
help her light the candles, and, since she was the
Queen of the Sabbath, she was allowed to decide,
of course. While the children were eating all the
good things, Miriam told them what she and
Daniel had seen. And Daniel—well, he was so
pleased, he almost laughed aloud.

"I did it, I did it," he thought. "Now Miriam is
not angry, sad or lonely anymore. Now she likes
being 'together.' "

The next morning, Aunt Rachel, who had the
night watch, asked Miriam what she had been
dreaming about during the night. "It must have
been something very nice," said Aunt Rachel. "You
laughed in your sleep."

Miriam remembered what she had dreamed,
but she would not tell. It was her secret, and a very
good secret, too.

Can you guess what it was?

In America Today

No, No, Not Haman

by Lilly S. Routtenberg

*What can David do? He refuses to be Haman
in the family Purim play. No one else wants to take
the villain's part, either.*

*Meet a foolish king, a beautiful queen, and
more than one hero in this story of a Purim play
that almost didn't take place.*

David ran to the kitchen. "Nobody wants to
be Haman," he cried out.

His mother was busy baking. She stopped
rolling out the dough and asked, "What's the matter, David?"

"They want me to be Haman in the play. The
one we're going to do for our family Purim party
next week."

"But David, if you children plan to present the
story of Purim, well, I guess someone will have to
play the role of Haman. Haman is a very important
character in the Purim story."

"I know, but Haman was wicked, and no one
likes a wicked person."

"Here, David, have a hamantash. Tell me if it's good."

"It's great," said David, his mouth full of the triangular, prune-filled pastry.

"Now, sit down and tell me all about it." Mother pulled up a chair for David.

He wiped his mouth, gave a deep sigh, and said, "Well, you know that last night Daddy told us why we celebrate the holiday of Purim."

"And did you like the story?"

"Oh, yes, it's all about a good guy and a bad guy, and the good guy wins."

"David, do you remember anything more than this business of good guys and bad guys?"

"Sure, there was Ahasuerus, the king of Persia—he was a nice guy. There was Mordecai, the old Jew who was Esther's cousin—he was a very, very good guy. Then there was beautiful Esther, who was chosen to be the queen. She saved all the Jews. But Haman, he was terrible, such a wicked man. I don't want to be him!"

David's sister and his three brothers came tramping noisily into the kitchen. Aaron, the oldest, said, "Where's David? David, we need you. We can't put on a Purim play without a Haman."

David faced them bravely and declared, "I'm not going to be Haman, and I don't want to be in your old play and that's all!"

"Oh, come on, David," said his sister, Yael. "It's all just pretend."

"No, it isn't. No one likes Haman, even in a play."

"We all know you're not wicked. We know what a great guy you are. Come on, be a sport," Alex pleaded.

"I am a sport but it's not fair. When Grandma and Grandpa and our aunts and uncles and cousins come to see the play, they'll love Yael because she's the queen; they'll like Alex because he's the king. And Aaron is Mordecai—everyone will love him. But no one will like me, because I'm Haman. I won't be Haman and you can't make me!"

"Children, please, let me finish baking. I still have to prepare another batch of hamantashen, so go back to the playroom and try to settle this among yourselves."

Dutifully, they marched out of the kitchen. Four-year-old Noam followed as fast as his little legs could take him.

They were all very serious as they settled themselves in a circle on the floor. They looked at each other. There was silence. Each one was thinking the same thought—no one wanted to be Haman!

Aaron spoke first, "Look here, I'm the oldest, so I should be Mordecai."

"And I must be the queen," said Yael, "because I'm the only girl."

"And I was the king last year in our Hebrew School Purim play," said Alex.

"So what?" asked David.

"So Mommy and Daddy thought I was very good—so I should be king again. You see, David, you'll just have to be Haman."

"No, No, I don't want to be Haman," said David firmly.

Suddenly, a thin little voice piped up. "I want to be Haman." It was Noam, looking very happy and pleased with himself.

"You want to be Haman?" asked David in surprise.

"Yes, I'm Haman," giggled Noam.

The children smiled, then laughed. Alex hugged Noam. Soon they were serious once more. What were they to do? Their whole family would be at the Purim *seudah*, the festive holiday meal, and they had decided to act out the story of Purim. It could be such fun.

"Well," said Aaron, "now that we have a Haman, we can go ahead with the play."

Alex shook his head sadly. "What can we do with a Haman that can't learn the lines of the play?"

A heavy gloom settled on the small group. After all, what's a Purim play without a Haman?

"I've got it!" shouted Aaron. "I've got it! It's simple."

They all looked at Aaron, "Come on, tell us."

"What do you do if you can't have a play with speaking parts? It's simple. You have one without speaking parts!"

"Oh, yeah?"

"Yeah—we'll make it a pantomime."

"A pant, a pantomime, what's that?" asked David.

"Well, you see, someone reads the story off stage, and the actors, dressed in costumes, act out the story as it is read."

"Oh, Aaron, you're wonderful," said Yael happily.

"You see how easy it can be?" Aaron said. "Now, David, since you're not in the play, you'll be the reader of the story. Let's try it out now."

David looked startled. "Does that mean that I won't be on the stage? And no one will see me?"

Aaron was firm, "That's right, since you won't be Haman, the least you can do is read the story."

David felt cornered. There was no way out of it. Yael gave him her Purim storybook and David began to read. With a little help, Noam managed to act the part of Haman. They all agreed that the pantomime would not be difficult to put on. It might even turn out to be a great success.

"Now we have to think about costumes," said Alex. "What should we wear?"

"I can make the crowns for the king and the queen," said Yael. "I know exactly what I'll wear— Mommy's old evening gown, the one she gave me for playing."

The Mordecai of the play said, "I can wear my choir robe. I think I'd like a beard. I'll bet I can make one out of cotton."

The thought of such a beard made them all laugh. All, that is, except David. He wasn't getting much fun out of this conversation. Alex felt that Daddy's blue velvet robe would be just right for the king. He suggested that Noam wear his striped pajama top, with a red sash and a three-cornered hat.

"I can make such a hat, and I think I'll draw a villain's moustache on him, to make him look really wicked," said Yael.

More laughter, all around, except David. Poor David. He sat there listening and wondering. Would there be a special costume for a reader? He shrugged his shoulders. What for? "No one will see me anyway," he thought.

"We're all set, and tomorrow we'll have a dress rehearsal after school," announced Aaron.

The next day, they all hurried home from school. Out came the robes, hats, sashes, and crowns. The scene was set with two armchairs for thrones. When all was ready, Aaron gave the signal, "Okay, David, start reading."

David began, "A long, long time ago, in the land of Persia, there ruled a king called Ahasuerus."

David continued to read. The actors were playing out their parts with more assurance this time.

That night, David could not fall asleep. He kept thinking about the play. The others had the roles they liked. Why couldn't he be on stage, too? He decided that he would read his part with real dramatic effect, so everyone would be impressed with his performance.

He got out of bed, tiptoed to Yael's room, and took the Purim book off the shelf. Returning to his room, he read the story and studied the pictures. Suddenly, he got an idea. "Yes, yes, that's what I'll do," he thought. Still smiling, he put out the light, turned on his side, and fell asleep.

The following evening, the family went to the synagogue to hear the story of Esther read from the Megillah, the handwritten Hebrew scroll that tells the Biblical story of Purim. The synagogue was filled with many people. Each child had a gragger, or some other kind of noisemaker. Whenever the reader of the Megillah scroll mentioned Haman's name, graggers twirled, horns blew, feet stamped. It was fun night in the synagogue, this one night of the year.

The next day, when the children came home from school, they saw the big table in the dining room, set for the Purim *seudah*. They could hardly wait for the party to begin.

In the early evening, the guests arrived, with *shalah manot*, gifts for all the children. The children gave out plates and baskets of hamantashen and candy. Each child also put part of his allowance in the charity box, as *shalah manot* for the poor. Everyone was happy, even David.

After the exchange of gifts, family and guests sat around the table, enjoying the different kinds of hamantashen. Some were filled with poppyseeds and honey, some with nuts and raisins, and some with jam. They all sang jolly Purim songs.

Then Aaron invited everyone into the living room. The children went to their rooms to put on their costumes while David cleared part of the living room, creating a kind of stage.

Daddy said, "Ladies and Gentlemen, your attention, please." All conversation stopped. He continued, "You are about to see the story of Purim presented by our children—Aaron, Alex, Yael, David, and Noam. Okay, kids, let's go!"

David's voice could be heard saying, "A long, long time ago in the land of Persia, it came to pass in the city of Shushan, that there ruled a king whose name was Ahasuerus. The king's prime minister was a very important man. His name was Haman. He was feared by all. He ordered everyone to bow down to him."

Daddy thought David's voice sounded strange. He looked around, but David was nowhere in sight. He looked toward the hall, no David. He looked around the room again—and then he saw it. The tape recorder! There it was, under a large chair in the corner of the room. "Aha, David never did want to be the reader so he found a way out. Pretty clever," Daddy thought. "But where is David now?"

David's voice was saying, "Messengers had been sent throughout the length and breadth of the entire kingdom to search for the most beautiful girl in all the land. At last they found her. Her name was Esther. They brought her before the king. When the king saw Esther, he was very pleased. He decided to make her his queen."

As he went on, the actors entered on cue. Then he got to the part about the king's wish to honor

Esther's cousin, Mordecai. "One night, the king was unable to fall asleep. He reached for his book of Chronicles and read of an event that had occurred a few months before. A man named Mordecai had saved his life!

He called his chamberlain and asked him, 'What has been done to reward Mordecai for saving my life?'

The chamberlain replied, 'Nothing, your Majesty.'

The king was angry. The following morning he sent for Haman and asked him, 'What do you think should be done for the man whom I wish to honor?'

Haman was sure that the king wished to honor him, so he answered, 'Dress him in royal robes, seat him on one of the king's finest horses, and let heralds lead him through the streets of Shushan.'

The king agreed, 'Bring the finest horse from the royal stable. See that Mordecai is seated on my best horse,' he said. 'Then you, Haman, lead him through the streets of Shushan.' Haman was disappointed. He was also very, very angry—at Mordecai and all the other Jews."

At that moment, Haman appeared, leading a horse. Well, a sort of a horse. Someone was dressed up in brown pajamas with brown socks on all four "feet." A horse face was painted on the paper bag on his head. A tail made of black yarn swished back and forth as the horse walked around on all fours.

The reader's voice called, "This is the man

whom the king wishes to honor!" Mordecai jumped
in surprise, but he proceeded to act his part, strad-
dling the horse and trying to look dignified. The
audience was delighted.

David's voice sounded like a real villain as he
told about Haman's conversation with the king,
"There is a certain people in the land whose reli-
gion is unlike any other. They call themselves
Jews. Let the Jews be destroyed."

Queen Esther waved her arms in a grand
gesture that almost knocked off her paper crown.

David's voice continued, "The king said to
Esther, 'Whatever you wish my Queen, I shall give
you, even if you ask for half my kingdom.'

'Oh my king, I must tell you that I and my
people are in grave danger. We are to be destroyed.'

King Ahasuerus was astonished. 'Who dares to
do this to you, and who are your people?'

Esther pointed to Haman and said, 'It is this
man, Haman, who has sworn to destroy the Jews in
your kingdom, and they are my people.'

'What?' shouted the King, 'You? My most
trusted servant?'

Haman fell at the feet of the king, asking for
forgiveness. But the king said to him, 'For this you
shall be killed. The Jews are saved!' "

The voice of the reader concluded the play,
"For sorrow was changed to great joy and the Jews
had light and joy and honor. Ever since, the Jewish
people have celebrated the fourteenth of Adar as
the happy holiday of Purim."

When the pantomime had ended, there was much applause. Haman and the horse returned to the room, greeted by more applause. They all bowed. Even the horse crossed one leg over the other, as circus horses do when they take a bow. Then the horse removed the paper bag from his head. The horse was David!

All the children wanted a ride on the human horse. David didn't mind; he liked being the most popular member of the cast. He gave the first ride to Noam, who looked very pleased with himself.

"Say, David, you were great!" exclaimed Alex. "How did you ever think up the horse?"

"Well, you see," said David, "I wanted to be in the play, too. So, I taped the story so I could be free to play the horse. My only problem was teaching Noam what to do and making sure he would keep my secret."

"But your costume, you really looked like a horse, sort of," Yael said.

"You did, you really did," Alex agreed.

"It was fun. I think I want to be the horse again next year."

"No," said Aaron, "I'm the oldest, so I think I should be the horse."

"But I'm bigger than you are, Aaron, so I think that I should be the horse," said Alex.

"Oh, dear," said Mommy, "Now it's not 'nobody wants to be Haman,' but everybody wants to be the horse. Thank goodness there's a whole year to solve this new problem."

The Sticky Surprise
by David A. Adler

*Something was wrong. The dough kept rising
and rising. Sharon and Michael planned a Passover
treat for their father, but this was not what they
expected.*

*Who knew the secret recipe for matzah that
could turn a bad surprise into a good surprise?*

Michael looked out the window of the sixth-
floor apartment. He often saw fire engines racing
to a fire, police cars chasing a speeding driver, and
on Thanksgiving Day, he watched the Macy's pa-
rade. But today there was nothing to see.

He walked quietly behind his sister and
watched as she did her homework. She kept turning pages, and reading, and writing, and turning
more pages. "How much longer, Sharon?"

She wrote a few more sentences as Michael
watched. Then she put her pencil down. "OK,
what do you want to do?"

"How about finishing that big jigsaw puzzle?"

"You can do that by yourself."

"Then how about playing Monopoly? I can't do that by myself."

"You left some property cards in your shirt pocket, remember? They got all crumpled up in the washing machine." Sharon thought for a minute. "Maybe we can think of something to surprise Daddy."

"We can vacuum the rugs or do the laundry," Michael suggested.

"No, no, I mean really surprise Daddy. Oh, I know," said Sharon, "Passover is in three weeks. Before Mommy was so ill, she used to bake matzah for the Seder. I think Dad will miss her homemade matzah. Come on, we'll look in the cookbook for a matzah recipe. We'll bake some to surprise Dad."

In the cookbook index, recipes were listed for macaroons, macaroon pudding, mashed potatoes, marzipan, matzah balls, and matzah brei. But there was no recipe for matzah. Sharon closed the cookbook.

"I think I know why there's no recipe for matzah. It's because you don't need a special matzah recipe."

"Why not?"

"We eat matzah because Jews ate matzah when they escaped from Egypt, right?"

"Yeah, right."

"They ate matzah because they were in a rush. They had to keep running. If they stayed in one place too long the Egyptians would have captured them and brought them back to slavery."

"So, what's all that got to do with there being no matzah recipe?"

"The Jews really made dough for bread. Because they were in a rush, they baked it without giving it a chance to rise. Matzah is really just bread that wasn't given a chance to rise. So if we use a bread recipe and don't give the dough a chance to rise, we'll have matzah!"

Sharon found a recipe for bread in the cookbook. She gathered the ingredients: flour, water, eggs, sugar and yeast. She read the cookbook instructions carefully and told Michael what to do. He took out a large mixing bowl, a wooden spoon, and measuring cups. He washed everything in warm water. Then, with his sister watching, Michael took out four large cookie trays and covered them with aluminum foil.

"Now we're ready," Sharon said. "As soon as I mix the dough, I'll put some on each tray. Then you help me flatten it. When we're finished, I'll put the dough in the oven. We have to work fast. We can't give it any time to rise."

Quickly, Sharon measured flour, water, eggs, and sugar into the mixing bowl. The recipe called for two compressed cakes of yeast. She could only find small foil envelopes of yeast. Cakes are rather large, Sharon thought. It would take hundreds of small foil envelopes like these to equal the size of just one cake. There was no time to go next door to borrow two cakes of yeast, so Sharon emptied the twelve small envelopes and poured them into the mixing bowl.

When the dough was all mixed, Michael helped· her flatten out eight matzahs, two on each tray. Sharon put them in the oven and set the timer to ring when the matzahs would be finished. "Now we wait," she told Michael, "Soon we'll have matzah."

They sat for a while and waited. Then Sharon jumped up. "I forgot to turn on the oven." She turned the oven on and set the temperature at 375°.

The timer rang. Michael got up to open the oven. "Wait, it's too early," Sharon yelled. "We never reset the timer."

But Michael didn't wait. Sharon watched as he took a potholder and carefully opened the oven. What they saw inside was not matzah. The dough on all the trays had puffed up like balloons. The dough on the lower trays was sticking to the bottom of the upper trays. Dough was hanging from the sides and top of the oven. Even as they watched, the dough seemed to grow.

"What a mess," Sharon said. "We have to get it out of the oven."

"Can't we just stick pins in it?" Michael asked.

Sharon didn't seem to hear him. She was running all over the apartment collecting newspapers to spread over the kitchen counters and the floor. When she returned to the kitchen, she looked at

Michael. Dough was hanging from his hands and from his shirt. He scratched his head. Now there was dough in his hair.

"What happened to you?"

"Well, I poked my fingers in the bubbles to make them go down. I guess that didn't work."

"Now we have to clean the oven *and* you. Just be careful, Michael. Don't touch anything until you get all that dough off."

Michael pulled the large pieces of dough off his hands and shirt. When he finished, Sharon was still busy spreading newspapers over the counters. Michael turned off the oven and looked inside. Each shelf was one mass of dough. The walls and the inside roof of the oven were covered with the sticky dough.

"Now listen carefully," Sharon told Michael. "I'm going to start taking the dough out of the oven and put it into the newspapers. You wrap it up and, as soon as you finish a bundle, take it and throw it down the incinerator. If we work quickly, maybe we can finish before Dad comes home."

Sharon reached into the oven and brought out a handful of dough. She tried to get the dough off her hands and onto the newspaper. It took time. When she took the dough off one hand, it stuck to the other. When she rolled up her sleeves, dough stuck to her blouse. When the newspaper was covered with dough, Michael wrapped it up. He ran from the kitchen, through the living room, and out of the apartment. Some dough dripped as he

ran. After he carried a few bundles, there was a
sticky trail of dough from the kitchen, through the
living room and hall, out the apartment front door
all the way to the incinerator room.

While Michael was carrying the ninth bundle,
the door opened. Mr. Binder stood there silently
and looked at his son. "What exactly are you
carrying? Whatever it is, it's dripping all over the
rug."

Then Sharon came out of the kitchen. Her
arms, face, and blouse were covered with dough.

While Mr. Binder stood there with his coat and
hat on, Sharon told him what had happened. When
he heard how the dough kept rising and rising, he
started to laugh. When Sharon finished explaining,
he said, "Now go back into the kitchen and don't
touch anything. I'll change into some old clothes
and help you clean up."

When everything and everyone were finally
clean, Mr. Binder said, "You surprised me today.
Tomorrow, after school, I'll try to have a good
surprise ready for you."

The next day, Sharon and Michael hurried
home after school. Their father was waiting for
them downstairs in the lobby of their apartment
building. Together they walked to the subway
station. During the long ride, Mr. Binder would not
tell Sharon or Michael where he was taking them.

When they came out of the station, nothing
looked familiar. There were stores along both sides
of the street. In front of many of the stores were

tables covered with records, jewelry, toys, and clothing. People surrounded the tables looking for bargains. Other people pushed past the shoppers. Radios were playing. Babies were crying. Mr. Binder held on to Sharon and Michael and led them through the crowd.

At the first corner they turned onto a smaller, quieter street. Mr. Binder stopped in front of a very old store. "Well," he said, "here we are."

Inside, the store was empty. Mr. Binder took Sharon and Michael behind the counter and into a large back room. They saw people working at a long table covered with paper. One of the men opened an oven door. Michael looked inside. "Matzah!" he shouted. "They're baking matzah!"

Mr. Binder walked over to the man and spoke to him softly.

"So," the man said to Sharon and Michael. "Your father says you also bake matzah."

"Well, we tried," Sharon told him. "We made dough and flattened it out, but when we put it in the oven, it kept rising and rising."

"Hmmm," the man said. "What was your dough made from?"

"Flour, water, eggs, sugar and yeast."

"YEAST!" the man exclaimed, "yeast! Never use yeast in matzah. Yeast makes dough rise. Here we use just flour and water."

Sharon and Michael followed him to a sink. As the man walked he mumbled "yeast" a few times and laughed to himself.

"Every eighteen minutes we wash everything," the man told them. "Maybe a little dough is left from matzah that we already baked. That dough has had time to rise. After eighteen minutes, it's really bread dough and we can't let it get mixed in with our matzah. We wash our hands for the same reason. We are very careful with the matzah we bake for Passover."

Once their hands were washed, Sharon and Michael sat next to each other at the table. The man brought them each some dough. With a rolling pin, they flattened it and then pressed a very large cookie cutter on the flattened dough. Now the dough was a perfect circle.

"Hold this by the handle," the man said to Sharon. He gave her a large round utensil. There was a handle on one side. On the other side, there were hundreds of sharp points.

"Stamp your matzah once with this," the man told Sharon. "This makes holes in the matzah so that it won't rise." Sharon stamped her matzah and then Michael did the same to his.

"Now I'll bake your matzahs," the man said. "We'll see if they rise with *my* recipe."

The matzahs didn't rise. After the matzahs cooled, the man wrapped them carefully. Sharon and Michael took turns carrying the package home.

At the Seder, three weeks later, Mr. Binder pointed proudly to the top two matzahs on the Seder plate. "You know," he told their guests, "Sharon and Michael baked these."

"Tell us how," their guests insisted.

Michael looked at Sharon and laughed. "Without yeast," he said, "without yeast!"

Glossary

Aaron the elder brother of Moses, and the first high priest of the Jewish people.

abba the Hebrew word for father.

Amen "May it be so!" Hebrew word to express agreement with a prayer or good wish.

Bar Mitzvah the ceremony marking a boy's growth into manhood at age thirteen.

Cohan a descendant of Aaron of priestly rank. Also spelled *Cohen.*

czar the ruler of Russia who had great power over the Russian people.

109

DAN an Israeli bus company.

droshky a low, open carriage with a bench for passengers, used in Russia.

Ellis Island a small island near New York City, once used as a center for people arriving in America as immigrants.

felafel deep-fried balls of mashed chickpeas and spices. A popular snack in Israel, usually eaten with pita bread.

Galilee the northern region of Israel.

gragger a noisemaker used on Purim to drown out the name of the villain Haman during the Megillah reading in the synagogue.

gulden gold or silver coins of the Netherlands, Germany, and Austria.

hamantashen triangular pastries filled with prunes, poppyseed, or fruit jam for the Purim holiday. The shape recalls the three-cornered hat worn by Haman.

Jerusalem the capital of Israel—an old, holy, and beautiful city.

kibbutz an Israeli farm where people live as one big family, working together and sharing what they have. Boys and girls live with children of their own age instead of with their parents.

kopeck a Russian coin. Also spelled *kopek*.

matzah a flat sheet of unleavened bread, similar to a cracker, made of flour and water. During Passover, matzah is eaten in place of fermented bread made with yeast. This commemorates the exodus of the Jews from Egypt, when their bread was made hastily without enough time to rise.

Megillah the handwritten Hebrew scroll of the Biblical Book of Esther, read on Purim.

Passover the holiday celebrating the liberation of the Jewish people from slavery in Egypt. Passover occurs in the spring, the fourteenth of Nisan on the Hebrew calendar. It is observed for eight days, with a Seder on the first two nights and eating matzah throughout the holiday.

P'Idyon Ha-Ben "redemption of the firstborn," ceremony for the firstborn son on the thirty-first day after his birth. In Biblical times, the firstborn son was dedicated to the priesthood. Later, members of the tribe of Levi were chosen to replace the firstborn of other tribes. The baby is redeemed from serving in the Temple by payment of five shekels to a Cohan, then the money is given to charity.

pita flat, round bread.

pontussel Polish word for cloth slippers.

Purim the joyous holiday celebrating the downfall of Haman and the saving of the Jews of Persia by Queen Esther and her cousin, Mordecai. Purim occurs in March, the fourteenth of Adar on the Hebrew calendar. It is observed with plays, costumes, exchange of gifts, and lots of noise and merriment.

Sabbath the seventh day of the week, Saturday, set aside for resting from work and everyday concerns. The Sabbath is ushered in when candles are lit at home. Blessings and prayers are said at home and in the synagogue.

sabra a cactus plant that grows in Israel—tough and prickly on the outside, but tender and sweet inside. People born in Israel are called Sabras.

samovar a metal urn, with a spigot, for heating water to make tea.

Seder the Hebrew word for "order," the home service and meal conducted according to a fixed order on the first two nights of Passover.

seudah a festive holiday meal.

shalah manot an exchange of gifts on Purim, usually plates and baskets of hamantashen and sweets. Contributions to charity are also an important Purim tradition.

shalom the Hebrew word for "peace," a greeting used for both hello and goodbye.

shekel a half-ounce silver coin, slightly larger in size than an American half-dollar. For a *P'Idyon Ha-Ben* ceremony today, five silver dollars are used.

synagogue the Jewish house of prayer and study.

tallis the fringed prayer-shawl worn by men when praying at home or in the synagogue. Also spelled *tallit*.

Talmud books of rabbinic literature containing commentaries on the Bible and traditional Jewish law and lore.

todah rabah Hebrew for "thank you very much."

Warsaw the capital of Poland.